# BOOBY HATCH

## by Betsy Lewin

CLARION BOOKS/New York

Pépe is born.
The first thing he sees is a pair of bright blue feet.
His mama and papa are blue-footed boobies.

They feed Pépe fish from the sea,
and soon he is a little cloud of downy feathers.

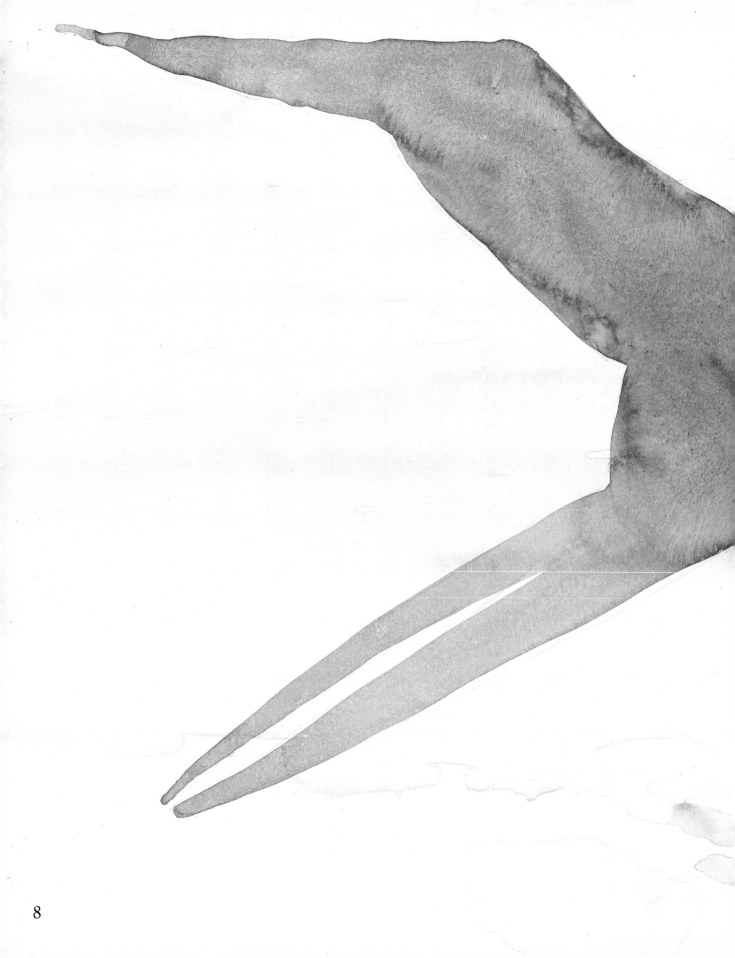

There is danger in the sky.

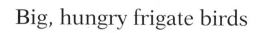

Big, hungry frigate birds

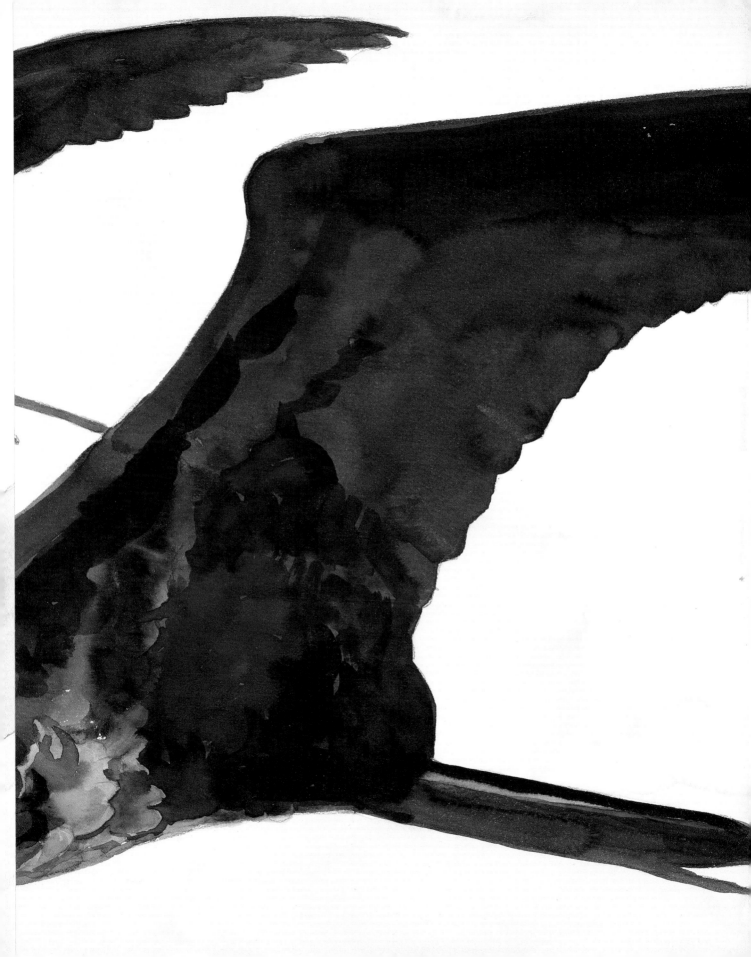

Lizards that live on land
and iguanas that live in the sea share Pépe's island.
So do the big, sleek sea lions that roll in the surf
and sun themselves on the rocky shore.

Pépe looks up at the wide, blue sky and flaps his wings. But his feet will not leave the ground. Not yet.

18

Then one day he flaps his wings
and this time they lift him high on the wind
to join a flock of his kind.

The leader whistles, and Pépe dives for his dinner
with the flock.

Now Pépe's feet are blue—bluer than the sky and the sea.
In the busy booby crowd one day, Pépe and Tina meet.
Tina curtsies and Pépe bows.

They dance,

and they dance,

and they show off their big, blue feet.

Then they point at the ground
where their nest will be.

And soon a little white egg will sit
in a circle of stones,
on a tiny island,
in a vast blue sea.

This story is about just one little booby, though
blue-footed boobies usually lay two to three eggs.

The iguanas in this book are marine iguanas,
and the crabs are called Sally Lightfoots.
The land lizard is called a lava lizard.
The little gray finches are Darwin's finches,
of which there are thirteen different species.
These animals are found only on the Galápagos Islands.

## The Galápagos Islands

MAINLAND ECUADOR →

Fernandina

James

Santa Cruz

Isabela

San Cristóbal

N

Floreana

Hood
(Pépe's island)

W          E

S